LISA RYAN CAMPBELL

Ex Factor

THE *ex* FILES

Cover design by Covers in Color
www.coversincolor.com

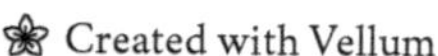 Created with Vellum

CHAPTER ONE

The air in the van was stifling, but none of the men spoke about it. This was too important of an operation to waste it complaining about irrelevant things like fresh air. David Holladay sat in the driver's seat with his binoculars lifted and spying on the target, Ian Nelson. His colleague sat to his right with a camera, ready to photograph whoever the target was about to meet in the busy San Francisco district.

Ian Nelson had been the agency's person of interest ever since the team got a tip from their inside man that Nelson had been spending more time away from crime boss Wesley Gannon's organization than usual. His movements in recent days had become suspicious, and the undercover operative believed he may be talking to someone on the outside.

"It's not one of us," David had said when he first heard the news. "If he hasn't turned informant, then who's he talking to?"

"I don't know," the undercover said. "But something must have happened between him and Gannon. He still appears loyal as ever, but something's off. He's a high-ranking member of Gannon's team and knows more than I do. It will be months, maybe years before Gannon trusts me enough to move me up. You should try bringing him in."

That was several weeks ago, and they had finally managed to get a warrant to track Nelson. Now, parked outside Hotel Nikko in Union Square, David's team sat, watched, and waited.

"Looks to me like he's meeting a girlfriend here," one of his men said from the back seat. "It's too fancy for a regular meet."

"Maybe that's his plan," David said, peering through the binoculars. "If Gannon is as paranoid as they say, he must have noticed his employee's change in attitude just like our informant and probably has men watching Nelson. This will throw them off."

The agent in the passenger seat suddenly sat up straight and raised his camera to eye level. "He's smiling at someone. I've got a woman walking up to him, African-American, mid-thirties, dark hair. She's smiling at him, too. This could be the girlfriend."

"Can you get her face?"

"She's turned away. I'll get her as soon as she... There!"

The photographer clicked multiple pictures as the woman slightly turned and her profile came into view.

David slowly lowered the binoculars and watched in disbelief at what he saw. The men in the van with him seemed to notice it at the exact moment he did, and everyone went quiet.

"It's your call, Holladay," one of the agents ventured to say. "What do you want to do?"

David's grip on the binoculars tightened. He was ready to jump out of the van, race across the street, and interrupt the two lovers greeting each other with an intimate embrace. But this case was his priority.

"Let it play," he said.

The photographer hesitated for only a second and then resumed capturing pictures of Ian Nelson walking arm in arm into the hotel with David's ex-wife.

CHAPTER TWO

Six months later…

Parker awoke, sensing the car had come to a stop. She looked around and frowned and then turned to face David, not at all recognizing her surroundings as the tree-lined neighborhood she called home.

"Where are we?"

He gave her one fleeting glance and then climbed out of the car without a word, and she stared after him as he walked with steady purpose to a brightly lit office. Her eyes moved along the one-story building to a sign, tall and large enough to be seen by motorists passing along the highway.

Willow Creek Motel.

Where the hell was Willow Creek, and why were they stopping here?

She counted fourteen rooms in an L-shaped structure, all on one level. It was nothing fancy, but she figured it was the kind of place that catered to those who needed one night of rest before continuing their journey.

David returned carrying a set of keys. As soon as he

opened the car door, she began peppering him with questions.

"What's going on? Why are we here?"

"We're staying here for the night," he said, angling the car in the direction of what she assumed would be their room.

"Why?"

"Why do you think? I'm tired."

"Then we should have stayed in Phoenix an extra day." *Like I suggested*, she thought wryly to herself.

He scoffed. "It's not exactly 'I told you so,' but it comes close, and under ten seconds, too. That's a record for you."

She ignored the bite in his tone. "If you're too tired, let me drive."

"You were buzzed from drinking at the reception."

"I slept it off. Besides, that was"—she paused to look at the dashboard clock—"four hours ago."

He pulled the car into one of many empty spaces in the small parking lot and switched off the ignition. "I already paid for the room. Let's get a few hours' sleep, and we can leave in the morning."

Parker wanted to say they could've spent a free night at the Phoenician and woken to a brunch given by the bride and groom but didn't want to rouse his temper any more. She could see he was already irritable, but dammit, so was she, and she had grown weary of catering to his mood swings. On a sigh, she got out of the car and grabbed her carry-on suitcase from the trunk. She doubted she'd need anything but a change of clothes and toiletries, but David was already standing by the open door, waiting for her with a very impatient look on his face, so she decided just to take the suitcase inside and sort through her things later.

She stepped past him through the open door, wheeling her suitcase behind her, gave the outdated furniture and carpeting a once-over, and wistfully thought of the Phoenician. Then she eyed the lone queen-sized bed and turned to see if David had noticed. He kicked the door shut behind him, looked at the bed and then her, and dropped his duffle into a chair.

"Sorry," he said, but from the subtle amusement in his light amber eyes, she guessed he wasn't sorry at all and was actually enjoying her discomfort.

"Are you hungry?" he asked. "I saw a convenience store about a mile back. I could go get us some sandwiches."

"David?"

He stopped at the door and turned to her. She stood completely still in the center of the room and tried to see through to his thoughts.

"Is there something you're not telling me?"

He seemed to take offense at her question but masked it quickly. "Everything's fine."

He turned and left, leaving Parker with the scent of her favorite cologne and his lie.

CHAPTER THREE

David wasn't really hungry, but he needed an excuse, any excuse, to get away from Parker and the close quarters they had been sharing for three days now. Friday morning, they'd driven the eleven hours to Phoenix and checked into the hotel that afternoon. That had not been such a problem since the room they'd shared was a suite with a pull-out couch that he used for the two nights they were there. But on Sunday, after Stephen and Marla's wedding, he was more than ready to leave. He used the excuse of needing to get back to San Francisco by Monday morning for a case he was working on, which was partially true. The other part of that truth was he'd grown tired of pretending in front of their friends that he and Parker were fucking perfect. Being surrounded by love and happiness made him resent the fact that he'd lost his own love and happiness, which, in turn, made him resent Parker.

So he'd whisked her away with the intention of bringing her home, but taking her home was the last the thing he'd planned to do. Right now, he was stalling for time.

The lights of the convenience store shone up ahead, and David slowed to pull in front of the blinking Open sign. He pulled out his cell phone again, highlighted the last call he'd made, and dialed it. It rang and rang, and with each sound in his ear, his irritation and worry increased. By the fifth ring, he pressed the *End* button and resisted smashing the device against the steering wheel.

He'd handpicked this team himself; each one had a stellar record and exuded competence and professionalism. If none of them was answering the damn phone, something had gone terribly wrong. As much as he wanted to go back, chances were good that he had now become a target, and standard protocol was he needed to stay low. That wouldn't be such a problem, except he had his ex-wife with him, and she was beginning to demand answers.

Movement out of the corner of his eye got David's attention, and he turned his head to see a man coming out of the convenience store. He turned toward David's car, gave him a brief glance, and then got into his own car and drove out of the lot. David kept his eye on the taillights but didn't feel any need for alarm. He let out a deep breath and told himself this wasn't the time to get paranoid about everyone that looked his way. He set his cell phone to the side, pulled down the visor, and took out the picture tucked inside, just as he always did when he felt he was losing control.

To an onlooker, he would have to explain where everything was, just as he had the nurse explain it to him, over and over again until he could trace the outline with his forefinger. He did so now without even thinking about it: head, nose, lips, arm, hand, leg, and foot. Just as he knew it would, the image calmed him, but there still remained that familiar ache that he would have to push through. He tucked the picture back into its hiding place, flipped the visor closed, and got out of his car to head inside the store.

He didn't want to leave Parker alone for too long but still dreaded having to go back to her and tell her more lies.

CHAPTER FOUR

Parker allowed the water to pour down her face and gave in to its heat. Closing her eyes, she imagined rough hands sliding down her back, slick from the soapy water. She didn't have to work hard to conjure an image. There was only one set of hands she'd grown comfortable and intimate with over the last six years. She could still feel those hands and warmed at the thought of what they could make her do.

The sound of the room door slamming shut was like ice water being thrown at her. David was back, and even though he played the starring role in her fantasies, she had to let it go. Despite the beautiful wedding weekend of their closest friends and the fact that they'd both played the loving married couple brilliantly, this was reality. Reality was bitterness with hurt feelings, hateful words that couldn't be snatched back, and a wall that took six years to build.

She shut off the shower nozzle and called out his name.

"Yeah, it's me," he called back in that sexy, deep tone.

They had to get back to San Francisco before she made a complete fool of herself. These three days of sharing space with him were dangerous for both her libido and her heart.

She quickly toweled herself dry and slipped on a nightshirt that stopped just at her knees. When she came out of the bathroom, he looked at her sleeping attire and then her before looking away. That glance in her direction was fleeting, but she saw the meaning in his eyes. They both knew she loved sleeping in panties and a tank top with no bra. She'd been free to do so in Phoenix because he chose to sleep in the hotel suite's pull out sofa while she'd had the bed to herself. But this small space didn't have a pull-out sofa, and she couldn't see herself sleeping in that kind of attire in the same bed with a man she'd served divorce papers to nearly a year ago.

He motioned to the convenience store plastic bag on a round table in the corner of the room.

"Don't expect too much."

She unwrapped the sandwiches and set aside the chips and bottled drinks as he used the bathroom and washed his hands. He toed off his shoes, unbuttoned the top two buttons of his dress shirt, and sat down to devour the meal. They ate in silence, trying to look everywhere else in the room but at each other, and it occurred to Parker how sad it was that the man she'd grown used to having around, the man she knew like the back of her own hand, was now a stranger.

"I liked your dress."

She stopped chewing, and the food in her mouth felt like clay as she struggled to swallow it down. He gave her another glance as if complimenting her had embarrassed him.

"I heard it was a tradition for bridesmaids to wear ugly dresses, but Marla did a good job. You looked great. I mean, you all looked great."

"Thank you," she said, braving a hint of a smile. "And that tradition is outdated. Brides realize if their friends don't look good, neither will the pictures. Besides, one of the best and stressful parts about planning a wedding is going out with your friends to shop for their dresses."

"Do you regret it?"

She picked up a chip but hesitated before putting it in her mouth.

Yes, I do regret serving you those papers, but you left me no choice, David.

"Regret what?"

"Not having the big wedding with all the trimmings."

They had eloped to Santa Barbara, something her sisters had been thoroughly pissed about, but she hadn't cared because she'd been in love. She looked at him and realized they were heading into dangerous territory.

"There's something you're not telling me," she said, putting the chip in her mouth.

He shook his head. "Good idea, let's change the subject."

"I want to know why you've been trying to push my buttons since we left Phoenix."

"I haven't. You fell asleep a half hour after we left, thanks to all the apple martinis you had."

That stung, but she ignored it and leaned forward in her chair.

"This is about work. What is it? Another case?"

"Lucky guess."

"Tell me."

He twisted the cap off his bottled water and took a long swig. He put the bottle down slowly and raised his eyes to look at her.

"I've lost contact with my team."

Parker kept her expression still. He didn't have to elaborate on that, because after a two-year courtship and a six-year marriage, she'd been privy to a lot of his cases. He never went into any detail, but she did know that part of his job involved keeping a confidential informant alive and safe to testify in court. That informant was usually guarded by a highly trained team of agents, and David oversaw the team. This was the first time she'd heard of him losing touch with them. She studied his posture, which was deceptively relaxed, but he was looking at the water bottle as if he wanted to hurl it across the room.

"How long has it been since you spoke with them?"

"Twelve hours."

"You were protecting someone?"

He nodded. "Not really protecting them. More like surveillance."

"Who?"

He gave her a look rife with skepticism.

"Do I really have to say off the record?"

"No, because I won't be giving you any details. You asked me what was wrong, and I told you. End of story."

"It doesn't explain why we have to stay here for the night. Tired, my ass."

He sighed. "Standard procedure. If my team has been compromised, I stay put until I can resume contact. I'm not taking you back to San Francisco until I know what's going on."

"Are we in danger?"

"No."

He said that just a bit too quickly for her, but she'd have to dwell on it later.

"Can you at least tell me who you're after?"

He didn't get a chance to respond because his phone began to chime, startling them both. David reached for it and answered with a brusque, "Holladay."

Parker couldn't detect the voice on the other end, but she studied David as he listened. His eyes flashed to her, and then he spoke to his caller.

"Give me a minute." Then he stood and addressed her. "Finish your dinner. I'll be right outside."

As soon as he closed the door behind him, Parker got up and fished her cell phone out of her purse and quickly made her own phone call.

CHAPTER FIVE

"Tell me what the fuck is going on. No one has been answering their phone."

He didn't tell David to calm down, relax, or anything else that would have made him blow a fuse. His director knew the circumstances, having been a field agent himself for many years.

"Those were my orders. We were busy fighting jurisdiction with the local cops."

"What happened?"

"Nelson. He was found in his home, shot through the head."

He pounded the roof of the car with his fist. "Shit! I knew we should have had more men on him."

"He refused witness protection, David. We can't waste resources on someone who hasn't agreed to cooperate with us."

"What about our undercover? Has he found anything?" David asked.

"Not enough to bring Gannon in. He's still small time and

hasn't gained enough trust to move higher in the organization. The director paused and then sighed. We don't have a choice anymore. You have to bring her in."

David leaned his body against the side of the car, feeling overwhelmed. He knew it would eventually come to this but had been trying to delay it for as long as possible. He dropped his head low, wishing he had the sonogram in his hands right now. He was reaching his limit and needed that gentle pull back to peace.

"I won't ask where you are, but wherever it is, you need to stay put. If they got to Nelson, it won't be long before they figure out her role in all of this."

David nodded, even though his director couldn't see the acknowledgment.

"I can play husband for a little while longer."

"How is Parker?"

"She hasn't changed."

"This is the first time you two have been together in nearly a year?"

"Yeah."

A heavy silence fell that carried a lot that was not being said.

"Stay safe," the director said. "I'll make contact as soon as I hear anything else."

David heard him speaking, but his attention was on the non-descript-looking sedan pulling into the parking lot. He recognized it instantly as the man he'd seen coming out of the convenience store. Twice in one night was making him suspicious. Yes, he could be a traveler, but his dark clothes, heavy boots, and tough-guy manner were all wrong. He was parked only a few feet away. When he got out of the car, he didn't so much as look at David, even though he must have seen him. Someone else may have made a corny joke like,

"Hey, are you following me?" or "We've got to stop meeting like this." Instead, this man seemed to be trying very hard not to look in his direction.

"David?"

"Yeah. I'll do that," he said and slowly disconnected the call.

* * *

The man called James waited until his target went inside his motel room before he soundlessly walked to a room just a few doors down and knocked. Dim light from a lamp inside partially filled the doorway. Without any words being exchanged, he slipped inside and closed the door behind him. He then turned to his companion who had let him inside.

"Where's Rivero?"

"Taking a leak," the man replied, gesturing to the bathroom in the corner of the room. "Did you see her?"

"Not her, but I saw that fed," James said, pulling a gun from his waist and handing it to his partner. "From the information we got, he's her ex-husband. What are the orders?"

His partner shrugged. "The boss says to do them both. Rivero and I will cover you."

"Get me a key."

"I'm on it," Rivero said as he emerged from the bathroom followed by the sound of flushing. In the next instant, he also pulled a gun from his waistband and twisted a silencer into the barrel.

The man addressed James. "No matter what happens, it's important she dies. The boss was clear on that. One bullet to the head."

James nodded. "Give it about an hour. He spotted me earlier at that 24-hour store a mile away and just now outside. I'm sure his cop instincts are on high alert. Let him relax a little."

They agreed and then nodded to Rivero, who cocked his gun and soundlessly left the room, heading in the direction of the manager's office.

CHAPTER SIX

Parker ended her phone conversation just seconds before David came into the room. She turned to him, knowing she looked guilty.

"Was that your director on the phone?" she asked, hoping he couldn't detect the quiver in her voice.

David gave an aloof nod, looking very distracted. She paused and then frowned as he kept his back to her, staring at the closed door.

"Did he give you any news about your team?" she ventured again.

He turned back around and gave her a brief glance. "He couldn't tell me much of anything."

He stepped around her and crossed to the small dining table where his food lay virtually untouched. He crumpled up the sandwich wrapper and stuffed it into the trash can.

"That was a lengthy conversation for not being told much of anything."

He whirled around to glare at her. "I don't owe you any explanations."

She stiffened. "Since I'm being forced to stay in this crappy motel instead of my own home, I think you do."

"You used to tell me about your dream of being an international correspondent, traveling all about the globe in the dirtiest places to get a good story, so don't pull that princess act with me. You're looking for an exclusive."

That hurt, but not because it wasn't true, because it was. What it told her was that he knew her like the back of his own hand, too.

She took a tentative step toward him. "I deserve that, but I'm genuinely concerned for you. I know you've been waiting for an opportunity like this for years. Personal feelings aside, I've always wanted the best for you."

He still regarded her with a hint of distrust, and she supposed it would always be there when he looked at her.

"Still no word," he said simply and then muttered, "I'm going to bed."

* * *

One quick tap to the door and James was letting Rivero back inside. Rivero said nothing but simply handed him a spare room key.

"We'll back you up," the man said again as if James needed more reassurance. "Try to keep the fed alive. Hopefully, he can tell us who the other snitch is in the organization."

"I'm not making any promises," James said.

It didn't matter if it was the three of them against one woman and a federal agent. They were still going in blind. He told them Holladay had seen him twice, but he didn't tell them he got the feeling the fed knew who he was and who he worked for. James would bet every last dollar he owned that Holladay was in his room preparing for an ambush.

James checked the clip of his gun. His partners could kiss his ass and so could Wes Gannon. He was the one taking all the risk. If he was going to walk into a cop's motel room at 3:00 a.m., he was going to be shooting—screw his orders.

CHAPTER SEVEN

When they'd first walked into the motel room, and he'd seen
Parker's face change to nervousness when she spotted the
lone queen-sized bed, he'd thought it was amusing. He'd
taken some strange pleasure in her discomfort, especially
since there had been no couch in sight, and he sure as hell
wasn't sleeping on the floor.

Now, lying back-to-back in the dark, careful not to touch
each other, he was the one feeling discomfort. He hadn't
shared the same bed with her in nearly a year, and even
though such a thing gave him pause, he shouldn't find her
warmth and her scent so enticing it nearly made him weep.
He'd taken such things for granted when he could look and
touch his fill of her. Now, everything about her was prohib-
ited and forbidden. It made him hard, but he refused to
move, knowing she'd understand just what he was trying to
relieve. Then she moved, and he sensed she was turning to
look at him. He kept his back turned, and his entire body
remained still.

What was she doing? What was she thinking? Did she
want to touch him as bad as he wanted to touch her? It

would be just his luck if she was staring and wondering what she ever saw in him. Maybe she was thinking about the baby.

Rather than drive himself crazy with these thoughts, David slowly turned his body until he was lying on his side and looking her directly in the eyes. She was fully awake, and even through the darkness, he could see her brown eyes widen as if she hadn't expected him to make that move. He waited her out, all the while reaching behind him toward the nightstand where his gun lay.

* * *

She hadn't expected him to turn around. She'd been content to just stare at the steady rise and fall of his bare back because it had been a long time since she'd been able to do this very thing. Now, that had been cut short, and she had to say something in order to explain why she was watching him. But something was off. He was looking at her, but his body seemed tensed as if he were waiting for something to happen.

She opened her mouth, ready to comment on this, but he stopped her by leaning close and putting his lips to hers. Her first reaction was to pull away from him, but the sensation of his kiss woke something inside her that she hadn't felt since the day he walked out of their home with his packed suitcases and boxes.

Without thinking, she put her hand to the side of his face. As soon as her fingers touched the stubble of his shaven face, he moved with lightning-fast reflexes and brought his arm up to clutch her about the waist. It caught Parker by surprise as she was roughly brought up against him, but it completely shocked her when in the next instant, he rolled atop her, and the two of them fell completely off the side of the bed.

David positioned himself so that he was underneath her

when they fell to the floor, but he didn't stop moving. He'd replaced his lips with the palm of his hand and motioned for her to keep quiet. That's when she heard it—the very faint sound of steps just outside their door. David slowly moved her off his body, and they both crouched on the side of the bed. She hadn't even known he'd grabbed for his gun when she saw him slowly cock the barrel and aim for the door. Parker's heart thrummed loud against her chest as she sank lower out of sight, waiting for whoever lurked behind that door to make their move.

Silence filled the air but was broken by the sound of an electronic key card slipping into the slot. Parker held back a gasp at the thought of someone going to all the trouble of getting a key to their room and entering while they would have been asleep. David gave her a slight nudge with his knee, willing her to keep calm, all the while keeping his eyes and gun trained on the door.

Suddenly, it burst open, and a rapid hail of muted gunfire hit the pillows and mattress. Parker kept her head hidden, willing herself not to scream. The gunman believed they were lying in bed, and for right now, that simple fact was saving their lives. The gunfire stopped as though their killer just realized his mistake. That slight hesitation must have been what David was waiting for because as soon as silence filled the room, he raised his gun and fired one, two, three times through the open door. The man fell back through the open door. David leaped up but stayed crouched down as he hugged the walls of the room to get to the door. With one hand steady on the pistol, he grabbed the dead man's leg and dragged him inside the room and slammed the door. With that, another hail of gunfire ripped through the now closed door, still muted from the silencers these men were obviously using. Parker couldn't believe there was more than one enemy out there. How many would they have to outshoot?

David backed away from the door and then put his body to the dresser where the TV rested and wedged the dresser against the door. Parker lay flat and belly-crawled to his duffle bag, where she knew he was bound to have a spare pistol. She rummaged through his clothes and toiletries until she found one with two spare clips. When the gunfire stopped again, she called to him.

"David," she whispered and tossed a clip to him.

"Stay down," he ordered and bent over the man to begin rummaging through his pockets.

Parker waited, keeping a worried glance toward the door with the dresser now barred against it. How long would that barrier stop them? What if they started shooting through the window?

David duck-walked his way toward her, and the two of them sat crouched beside the bed. "I'm going to try to get us out of here, but I need you to listen to me."

"Who are they?"

"Parker—"

"Who are they?" she asked again.

He shook his head. "I didn't find any ID, but my guess is they work for a crime boss based in San Francisco."

Parker didn't need him to elaborate further, but she couldn't let on she knew who he was talking about. Wesley Gannon.

CHAPTER EIGHT

David listened and exhaled a breath as he heard footsteps hurry away from the room. For now, the others who accompanied this dead one at his feet were retreating. But he didn't know how long they had. He had to get Parker out of here.

"Keep the lights off and get dressed," he said, pulling aside the curtains only slightly and risking a look outside. No one was in sight.

Chances were these men had rented a room and had gone back to rearm and re-strategize. David looked down and figured they'd sent their best gunman in to take care of Parker and him. Now that he was dead, they were probably tossing a coin to decide who would take the lead this time, now that the element of surprise was gone.

"Shit!"

"What is it?"

He turned to Parker, who was now fully dressed and holding his spare gun at her side. He didn't reply but stepped past her where his trousers and shirt lay tossed on a chair and put them on.

"David," she said with a hiss and exasperation filling her voice. "Why are these men after you?"

"I'll explain everything later."

She didn't say anything but moved with speed as she reached for her purse and pulled out her cell phone.

"What are you doing?" he asked.

"Calling the police."

"They won't get here in time. Besides, we're leaving now."

"How?"

He shrugged on his shirt and motioned for her to follow him into the bathroom, where a picture window sat between the shower and the vanity sink. It was small but still big enough to fit through. He had noticed this detail as soon as they entered the room that evening. After fifteen years on the job, it had become natural for him to look for all possible exits in any room.

"You're going out through here."

"What about you?"

"I'm going to cause a diversion out front so those assholes are paying attention to me."

"David—"

"I want you to run for those trees," he said, paying no heed to her objections. "Don't look back, no matter what you hear. Just keep moving."

He pulled his cell phone from his back pocket and handed it to her. "My director's number is programmed in there. If anything happens, you keep going and call him as soon as you can."

"Why don't you come with me?" she asked with a note of desperation in her voice.

Because he needed answers, and he didn't want her hanging around to see just how he got them.

"It's safer this way," he said. "I need you to trust me."

He watched as she searched his eyes in the dark, and he could see her mind was quickly working out any other plan that would suit her better than his.

"Trust me," he said again.

Finally, she nodded. "Make sure you find me."

CHAPTER NINE

Parker stood by the open doorway separating the bedroom from the bathroom. She watched as David moved toward the window and peeked out. He must have been satisfied with what he saw, because he then edged his way to the door, moved the dresser away from it, paused, and then slowly turned the knob. Before opening it, he looked her way and gave her a subtle nod.

She thought maybe she should say something like, "Be careful," or, "Stay safe," but none of those words felt right. What she really wanted to say was on the tip of her tongue and hadn't been uttered between them in a long time. She kept her mouth closed, turned, and bolted for the bathroom window. It opened easily, and she climbed her way through. But as soon as her feet touched the ground, she heard a rapid exchange of fire coming from the front of the motel. Her heart leaped to her throat, but she had to follow David's orders. The trees were well within sight, and if she ran, she knew she could make it, get lost in the darkness, and wait for him. But light coming from her left side caught her eye. It shone from the rear room of the manager's office. Was he in there? She had her phone with her, and David's contact at the DEA programmed in it. But, he needed help now. Maybe the manager had heard all the commotion and was on the phone with the police right now. She could go and lock herself in the office with him, and if he wasn't there, she could call the police and leave the phone off the hook. A small town like this, out in the middle of nowhere, it wouldn't take long for them to get here.

She looked to the trees once more and then was propelled into action by more gunfire. She ran for the office and burst through the door, not sure if someone was right behind her. She dropped to the floor and crawled her way to the back office. She turned the knob and pushed open the door. It barely budged. She shoved against it again, and it moved a half an inch. She looked behind her, feeling a sense of panic overwhelm her, but saw no one coming. She pushed harder, and the door opened enough that she could see what was blocking it.

A body lay on the floor, and blood was pooling around it. Parker backed away, putting a hand to her mouth to hold back the scream in her throat. She took several deep breaths, willing herself to get under control. David needed help. She could at least do this for him.

Biting back nausea, she pushed against the door one more time, moving the manager's heavy body out of the way. She peered inside the small office but didn't see anyone. Her eyes fell on the landline by the computer, and she stepped over his body and crossed to the phone, gripping the receiver like a lifeline. Raising it to her ear, she nearly let out a cry when she didn't hear a dial tone.

"Dammit!"

She could use her cell phone, but she'd need an address to give to the dispatch operator. Maybe all she needed was a business name. This was a rural area and the only motel for miles. What was the name again? Moving quickly, she pulled out her cell phone and raced from the office to the front where the motel sign would be. But she skidded to a halt when she saw the dark figure striding purposefully toward the office, a gun in his hand. Parker spotted the light switch and flipped it off, plunging her into darkness.

CHAPTER TEN

With Parker safely out of the way, David set about to get the answers he needed. Throughout their marriage, he'd done his best to shield her from the darker side of law enforcement or, more specifically, drug trafficking. He'd been content to let her believe that day in, and day out, he caught the bad guys and brought them to justice, without letting on that sometimes he had to be the bad guy in order to do so. He wanted always to remain the hero in her eyes, and he had until the day he decided to move out of their home.

He cracked open the door and swiftly moved outside, taking immediate cover behind his car. He peered over the hood and watched through the dimly lit parking lot for any sign of movement. The lights to the main office were still illuminated, which had been a careless move on their part. He was certain they'd done away with the manager, but they should have killed the lights, too. At least that's what David would have done to keep his target as blind as possible.

There. Ahead, he saw a figure hurrying away from him, nearly rounding the corner to the rear of the motel. Damn, he wasn't sure just how far Parker had managed to escape, but he couldn't let this asshole get around to the back and risk him seeing her running for the trees. It was a risk to himself because he wasn't sure how many of these guys there were and whether one of them had a bead on him right now. But this was Parker, and ex-wife or not, he wouldn't stop protecting her.

He rounded the hood of his car and trailed the man in stealth-like fashion until he was directly behind him. Just as he reached the rear of the property, David pushed the barrel of his gun into the back of the man's head.

"You move, you die."

The man froze and slowly raised his hands. David snatched the gun from his grasp, engaged the safety, and tucked it into the waistband of his pants.

"Who else is out here with you?" he asked, taking a look around.

"Just me," the man said in a gruff voice.

David dug the barrel in deeper, pushing the man's head forward. "You sure about that?"

"There were only two of us out here. You killed my partner."

"Who sent you?"

"You already know. And you may as well pull the trigger because if I tell you anything, I'm a dead man."

David reacted instantly, bringing the barrel of his gun down hard on the man's head, and he dropped to his knees. No, he wouldn't kill him, but he could make life very unpleasant for him.

"Goddamn," the man cried out. He put two fingers to his head, gingerly touching the wound that was now seeping blood down his face. He turned and stared up at David with murder in his eyes. David only pointed the gun, unmoved.

"How did he find us?"

"You really think you can keep her safe forever? That

snitch Nelson told her too much. Gannon wants her dead. You can stop me or my guys, but he'll just send more to replace us."

David knew he was right, but before he could question him any further, a shot fired from the front office, and it wasn't a silencer.

Parker?

The distraction was enough to take his attention off the man, and because of it, he nearly missed it when he grabbed for a hidden gun from an ankle holster. But David's reflexes were faster. As the gunman's hand came up to fire, David brought his own hand down hard against his wrist, knocking the gun from the man's grip. He then whipped the pistol against the man's face in quick succession until he fell back. He left the man unconscious on the ground and ran for the office, doing his best to keep his fear at bay.

CHAPTER ELEVEN

Parker crouched down in the corner of the room beside the dead manager's body and listened to the sound of her rapidly beating heart. He was coming through that door with only one purpose in mind, and she would have to kill him. The mere thought of killing another human made her nauseous and her pulse thrum faster. But he wouldn't think twice about killing her, so she had to shut off the compassionate side of her brain.

The crunch of his boots on gravel sounded louder as he approached the door of the back office. Too late, she realized she should've used something to barricade it. There was no time now. He turned the knob, but she'd at least had the foresight to lock the door.

Not a second later, he shot the lock off. Parker jumped and then pointed her gun at the door, ready to fire round after round into anything that moved. Then came the sound of a scuffle and a grunt, but no one came through the door. Parker nearly lowered her gun and then stopped as the door began to swing slowly open. She fired several times.

"Parker, it's me! I'm coming in!"

David.

She dropped her hand instantly. "I'm here in the corner."

He opened the door wider. His silhouette was backlit by the light of the parking lot, but Parker knew his stance and let out a heavy breath filled with relief.

He came forward and knelt down beside her. "Are you all right?"

"Yes. Are they all dead?"

"Two of them, including the one behind me, but there's one in the back of the motel knocked out."

"What if there are more?"

"That's a chance we'll have to take." He stood and offered his hand down to lift her up. "Let's get out of here."

CHAPTER TWELVE

Parker didn't have time to pay attention to the man outside the manager's office with his neck in an awkward position, or the man lying face-down on the ground several yards from their room. She especially didn't have time to look at the one with three bullet holes in his chest because David was ushering her around the room so fast, grabbing everything they came with.

"Make sure you don't forget anything," he said. "I'll keep watch outside."

So, she grabbed his and her things, sloppily stuffing them into the overnight bags. She hastily stepped past the fallen man, now bleeding over the carpet and tried not to shiver. After all, these men had come for David and would have killed her in the process. It was pointless to feel any kind of sympathy. David took the bags from her, threw them into the back seat of their car, and waited until she got in before climbing into the driver's seat.

"I'm surprised they didn't disable the car," he said, turning the ignition and listening to the engine roar to life.

"Maybe they were so confident in their mission that they didn't feel the need to," she said.

He eyed her quickly before turning to look behind him as he backed out of the motel parking lot. Parker watched in her side view mirror as the flashing vacancy sign grew farther away and didn't begin to breathe easier until it and its carnage were completely out of her line of sight. David waited until they were several miles away before calling the police. He gave the name and address of the motel, reported shots being fired, and then hung up as the dispatcher began asking him more questions. After that, nothing was said for a long time.

Parker was still amped up from the danger they'd just faced and found she couldn't keep still. Adrenaline had her squirming in her seat, constantly looking back for anyone that might be pursuing them.

"You can relax now," David said. "No one is after us."

"How do you know they didn't put a tracker on the car?"

"They didn't."

"Then how did they know where to find you?"

He stayed silent, and she got the feeling he really wanted her to shut up, but she couldn't, not after what happened back there.

"David, how did those men know where you were?"

"I told you to run for the trees."

"What?"

He looked at her now, and inside the dark car, she could see the anger falling over him like a blanket.

"I told you to run. I told you to get out of there and hide until I could find you."

She sighed. "I know."

"But you didn't. Why?"

"I thought the manager was still alive. I thought he'd have a landline that worked. The police could have come and—"

"But the landline was disconnected, wasn't it?"

"Yes."

"And the manager was dead, wasn't he?"

Parker tucked one leg underneath her and turned to face him. "How was I supposed to know any of that?"

"You didn't have to know because I knew."

"You could've told me."

He erupted. "I told you to run for the trees! For once, listen to me! I said run for the trees, don't take too many risks with your job, stop working so many hours—"

He stopped abruptly, turned to her, and then faced the dark road again, muttering curses to himself. But she'd heard enough, pulled back from him, and willed the tears to stay away.

"You do blame me, don't you?" she asked.

"No," he said quickly and then hit the steering wheel with an open palm. "Christ, I didn't mean… I wasn't talking about the baby."

But they both knew he was.

CHAPTER THIRTEEN

David kept his eyes straight ahead, not wanting to see the look in her eyes. What he said to her had meant to be something he'd take to his grave. He never wanted her to know that he blamed her for the baby; he never wanted to blame her at all, but it had been too fucking hard to go on believing what his parents and close friends said, "These things just happen." It had been a blow to hear he was not going to be a father, and it had been so easy to lay all the anger, hurt, and yes, blame, at Parker's feet. A lot easier than to look at himself in the mirror.

"Where are we going?"

He looked over at her, surprised to hear her speaking to him. After he'd said what he did about the baby, she'd closed up on him, and that had been forty-five minutes ago. It had become a typical rhythm leading up to the months before their separation: he'd say something hurtful, and she would shut down. Nothing ever got resolved.

"I don't want to take you home just yet. These people know you're with me, and since I just took out three of their men, they'll be looking for my head and would be glad to use you as bait. I need to find somewhere safe to lay low."

"Gypsy Bay," she said immediately.

He frowned. "Gypsy Bay? I thought you and your sisters sold that house months ago."

"We had a buyer, but the financing fell through. Then Tess started getting sentimental, saying it was wrong of us to sell the place where Mom and Dad spent their honeymoon. So we took it off the market." She cast a side glance his way. "No one knows about it."

"I don't want to get your sisters involved in this."

She scoffed. "They won't be there. We kept the house, but we never really get a chance to visit. Everyone is so busy with their own lives."

He gave it another moment's thought but couldn't come up with a better plan of his own. He checked his watch. "We should be there by morning. Try to get some sleep."

"Are you serious? We were nearly killed back there. I don't think I'll be able to sleep for a month."

He started to press the issue but was distracted when the display on her phone lit up, signaling she had a call. He hadn't realized until then that she'd been cradling her cell phone in her hands. Parker looked down immediately to see who was calling and then pressed the *Ignore* button.

"Who was that?"

She looked at him, and he got the feeling she wanted to tell him to mind his own business. Ex-husbands no longer had a right to question incoming calls. Still, he looked at her expectantly, waiting for an answer.

"My editor. I'm on deadline, and she's probably wondering where I am. I'll call her back later."

He didn't like the evasiveness in her tone, which made him wonder if what she was telling him was the truth. He let it go for the time being.

"You still haven't told me what's really going on here," she said.

"There's nothing more to tell. You know as much as I do now."

"I know your director said much more than you're telling me."

Apparently, the shock of danger and threat of death was slowly wearing off, and she could now get back to what she did best, which was finding answers.

He waited a beat before answering. Maybe he could get her to tell him something if he was more upfront with her. "We've been after a crime boss named Wes Gannon for years. Recently, we approached one of his men to turn informant for us, but he refused. We kept him on surveillance, but Gannon's men got to him."

"If he didn't turn informant, why was he killed?"

"It's the threat of turning informant."

Parker thought for a moment. "I've heard of Wes Gannon. But from my research, I see he's also a businessman. Who was the man you had on surveillance?"

He turned to her but didn't answer the question. Despite how angry he was with her and her stubbornness, she looked beautiful and sexy when she was trying to work out an angle. His eyes trailed down to her full, mouth-watering lips, and he recalled the moment just before all hell broke loose. He could tell himself he only kissed her to keep her quiet, but the truth was he missed her and needed to touch her. Even now, with her sitting so close to him, his hands itched to reach across the console and massage the back of her neck for her, which she was now rubbing. It was a telltale sign of the stress she was feeling.

"You really should try to get some sleep."

She turned to look out the window, watching the passing darkness. "I'll sleep when I know I'm safe."

That cut him deep. So deep he couldn't help himself. "You used to say I made you feel safe."

She let go a heavy breath and continued to stare out the window. "That was when you were around."

His jaw hardened, and his hands clenched around the steering wheel. Now would be a good time to count backward from ten, but he couldn't let that go.

"I never left you."

She whipped her head around, eyes flashing. "As much as you stayed away, you may as well have."

"We were fighting every day. It got too exhausting to be there."

"You mean to be near me."

"I'm not doing this, Parker. Rehashing what went wrong with our marriage is not my priority right now."

She looked away from him, and he heard what she said under her breath. "It never was."

CHAPTER FOURTEEN

For the second time in twenty-four hours, Parker felt the car pull to a stop and awoke, realizing she had actually slept. She looked across the seat at David, who turned to her with an unreadable expression on his face.

"We're here," he said simply.

Then she looked outside and smiled at the sight of the rising sun along the quiet, tree-lined street with brightly-painted homes where she and her family had spent summers during her childhood. David handed her a small white paper bag and a plastic bottle of orange juice.

"Blueberry muffin," he said. "It's not much for breakfast, but I don't want to go out until I call my director."

She nodded and looked up at the two-story bungalow from her youth. "We still keep a cleaning service, and there might be some canned food in the pantry."

"Okay. Let me go in first."

She frowned. "David, there's no way—"

"I'm sure it's fine, but humor me."

She sighed but nodded her agreement. He reached across

her, pulled open the glove compartment, and grabbed his gun and clip. He slipped the clip inside and climbed out of the car in one motion. He went around to the back, just as Parker knew he would, and was out of sight. Reluctantly, she had to admit to herself she appreciated his caution. She didn't believe anyone had managed to follow them here to the small coastal town, but it hadn't stopped the thought from entering her mind several times on the way here. She tried to peer through the shroud of bougainvillea bushes that surrounded the perimeter of the home but couldn't see David.

You used to say I made you feel safe.

Why didn't she tell him he still did make her feel safe? He'd been so angry with her for not following his orders, for not running away, but the truth was she had no doubt he would have been all right facing those men alone. She hadn't disobeyed him simply to find a telephone. She just wanted to stay near him, where she felt safe.

Her cell phone rang, breaking the silence. Parker jumped and quickly dug through her purse to get it and then glanced at the number on the display. She looked up, and when she didn't see David returning, answered the call.

"Hello?"

"Where have you been," her editor, Diane, asked. "I've grown a clump of gray hair worrying about you."

"I'm sorry," Parker said. "This is the first time I've been alone. I've been too busy trying to stay alive."

"What do you mean? What happened?"

"It's a long story. Suffice it to say I'm hiding out in my parents' summer house with my ex-husband."

A long silence came from the other end.

"Diane?"

"David is with you?"

"Yes, but that's not the problem. I haven't been able to get in contact with my source, and I'm afraid he might have skipped town on me."

A long sigh. "Yeah, well, that's why I've been calling you."

Parker sat up straight. "Have you heard from him?"

"No, but I have heard from the DEA, more specifically, my boss has, and they want the notes for your story."

"What? How did they even know about this?"

"It seems they're after Gannon, and they have reason to believe you have evidence to take him down."

"What if I do? It's my story."

"You and your story just became a part of their investigation. They came here talking about obstruction of justice and using a lot of other legal words. We got in touch with the legal department, but they basically said our hands are tied. We're now cooperating with the DEA."

"Are you kidding me? You're actually telling me to hand over the story?"

"We made a deal. We have forty-eight hours."

Parker leaned her head back against the headrest, resisting the urge to scream.

Diane sighed. "We had no other choice, Parker. They've been watching you for a long time."

"What? They've been watching me?"

"They know you've been meeting with your source. Hasn't David told you any of this?"

Parker looked up and saw David returning to the car, and she realized she'd been a complete fool. "No, he didn't. Look, I'll have to call you back."

She ended the call quickly and slid the phone to the side and out of sight just as David came to the open driver side window.

* * *

Diane called Parker's name twice before cursing and hanging up. After she disconnected, the man who had tapped Diane's desk phone line stopped the recording and turned to his partner.

"Find out where this summer house is and call in your best men. The boss wants this handled right this time. The woman needs to be dead by morning."

CHAPTER FIFTEEN

David ushered Parker inside and closed the door behind them. He immediately turned around, locked it, and looked out the front window through the drapes, all the while, checking the clip in his gun. When he was satisfied the street remained still and quiet, he turned from the window to find Parker staring at him. He knew she was working something out in her mind, so he stood there and waited her out.

"What have you done with him?"

"Who?"

"My source."

Silence.

"Did you arrest him? Put him in protective custody? I know you know about him, about everything, so just tell me—"

"He's dead."

She stared at him so long, he thought she wasn't really seeing him anymore.

"How—how did you..."

"We've been tracking you and Nelson for six months now. We know you two met up and that he gave you information about Gannon's organization. We got word from our undercover op that there was word spreading that someone was talking to the press. We approached your source, told him what we knew, and offered to let us put him in protective custody, but he refused. Last night, he was found dead."

Parker braced a shaky hand on the arm of the sofa and slowly sat down. David figured the best way to tell her this was to get it all out at once.

"We didn't think Gannon knew it was you his man spoke to, but I kept surveillance on you. It wasn't until we got to the motel that I was sure he knew about you."

She'd been staring at a spot on the coffee table in front of her but raised her head slowly at that last word.

"Are you saying those men came for me? I thought this all had to do with you and a CI."

"I said that because I wasn't sure how the DEA was going to pursue this."

"They want my notes, David. They want me to testify."

"I was told the same by my director last night."

"So the wedding was just a ruse to keep tabs on me? Did Stephen and Marla know about this too?"

"Stephen is my friend. He asked me to be his best man."

"But you knew I'd be there."

"I knew. That's why I suggested we take the trip to Phoenix together."

"To keep an eye on me."

"To keep you safe."

"To interrogate me."

Those had been his orders, but each time he got her alone, he couldn't do it. She wasn't just some journalist on the lead of a story, she was Parker, his ex-wife, who was now in the crosshairs of a very dangerous man.

"The motel was just a stalling tactic," he said. "I planned to tell you everything, but then those men came and plans changed."

She laughed with scorn. "I knew something was off when you agreed to go to the wedding with me. You hate weddings. I thought maybe…"

"What?"

"Nothing. It's stupid." She took a deep breath and shook her head as if to dislodge the thoughts entirely.

He watched as she rose from the sofa and took a seat at the dining table.

"Go ahead. Ask me whatever you want."

* * *

David ran his hands down his face in a gesture that was so familiar to her. He'd reached his limits of frustration, but she didn't know if it was because of her or this job. He didn't like having to interrogate her; she knew that. But she also knew he would do his duty.

"We should wait until we get back to San Francisco. You can have the attorney representing your newspaper sit with you."

"I'd rather get this over with. Just you and me."

He considered her for a moment longer and then nodded his head once and turned to pull a file folder out of the messenger bag he brought inside with him. He came forward, sat down across from her, and opened the folder. Without preamble, he took the first photograph out and pushed it toward her.

"Do you recognize this man?"

Parker looked at the picture for only a moment before responding. "Yes, that's Ian Nelson."

"Is it true that Mr. Nelson has been a source of information for you into Wesley Gannon's organization?"

Since the man was now dead, Parker answered truthfully. "Yes, Ian Nelson was my source."

David put another picture in front of her. "This was taken six months ago. Is it fair to say that was your first meeting with the victim?"

She stared down at the image of the two of them with their heads bent low at a coffee shop. It was night out, but the picture was clear, not mistaking the appearance of secrets being passed between them.

"Yes. He contacted me and said he was familiar with my work. He wanted a way to take Wes Gannon down without going to the cops. Apparently, Mr. Gannon had killed someone Ian loved, and he wanted revenge."

He stayed quiet, and Parker recognized the tactic as a way to encourage a witness to keep talking. It was no matter. She was still going to write her story, at least as a means of keeping her promise to Ian.

"We agreed that I wouldn't print the story until he was far away from California and Gannon's organization. So we met on multiple occasions, and he told me everything he knew."

"Where did you two meet?"

"Diners, mostly. Mall parking lots at night, any place that would give us some semblance of privacy."

"Hotel rooms?"

Diane was right. They had been tailing her every move. But before she could respond, David put another picture in front of her, only this time it hit the table with a slap.

"This was taken three weeks after your first meeting with Ian Nelson. The two of you entered Hotel Nikko in Union Square under an assumed name reserved by him and didn't come out until an hour and a half later."

She looked over the glossy color photo and into his eyes now clouded over with fury. "I know what it looks like."

He slapped another photo down. "Two weeks after that, same hotel."

"David—"

Another photograph. "This time, you go in together, arms locked."

"Please, let me explain."

"Explain why his arms are around your waist in this one."

"Wait a minute!" She held up both hands to stop him and stood from the table. "I didn't sleep with him. That's what you really want to ask me, isn't it?"

David remained still.

Parker let out a heavy sigh and looked down at the photograph of her smiling up at Ian with him leaning forward to kiss her temple as they entered through the double doors of Hotel Nikko. She knew exactly what it looked like: two lovers taking the afternoon off to enjoy each other's company. How could anyone even begin to guess that it was all for show?

"He told me Gannon was a paranoid man. He was always expecting the people in his organization would turn on him at any given moment. He thought that if maybe we posed as lovers, Gannon wouldn't look so hard at him for spending so much time with me."

She then lowered her voice to a near whisper. "You had already moved out by then, David. Our divorce was final. Believe me, I wouldn't have agreed to his terms if you and I were..."

"I know," he said suddenly and pushed away from the table to stand. "I know you wouldn't. He cursed under his breath. "I shouldn't have done this here. Not like this. This is supposed to be about Gannon not..."

He gestured a hand to all the pictures laid out on the table.

"It's okay."

"No, it's not. None of this is okay. You were right. I went to the wedding with you only to interrogate you. I would have turned down Stephen's offer to be his best man, otherwise."

"Because I would have been there?"

"Yeah. Because I didn't want to see how beautiful you would look. I didn't want the reminders of our own wedding day while I had a job to do."

She wondered if he realized what he'd said because, suddenly, the air in the room went still, taut with the admission that he still thought about their marriage as much as she did. For a long time, they just stared at each other until David took a step toward her.

"Tell me what you thought."

"What?"

Another step. "Why did you think I came with you to Phoenix?"

"It's not important."

"It is to me."

She looked everywhere but at him, suddenly feeling embarrassed by her thoughts.

"Tell me," he urged. He was now directly in front of her, using his finger and thumb to make her face him.

"I thought you wanted to be with me. I thought..."

He was so close now, she could practically feel the heat coming off him. He slowly lifted the edge of her shirt and caressed two fingers to her bare skin. "Go on."

Parker sighed. "I thought you missed me."

He had both hands on her waist now and brought her body firmly against his. He moved to her ear and bit the lobe gently.

"Ask me."

Her eyes closed to the sensations he was making her feel. "Ask you what?"

"Ask me if I missed you."

She opened her eyes and looked at him. "Did you miss me?"

* * *

He responded by covering her lips with his own, and the kiss was hot and devouring. He pulled her shirt up and over her head and watched as her dark hair tumbled free and framed her face. She was beautiful with the rays of the setting sun on her face, and he couldn't resist staring at her plump honey-colored breasts and dark nipples peeking from the violet lace bra she wore. She always thought her breasts were too big, but he never failed to assure her they were perfect for her and for him.

When he'd looked his fill, he took her by the hand and led her upstairs to the master bedroom. He was ready for her, but he wasn't going to rush a moment he'd been fantasizing about for the past year. For too many nights, he'd stayed awake in bed, rubbing his erection, thinking of her on top of him, him on top of her, him taking her from behind, him taking her from the side, and every other position they'd tried and that he could remember. Now, those nights were no longer just a part of his imagination. She was here and even better than he remembered.

"Get undressed," he commanded.

She obeyed by pulling her jeans over her full hips and ass and then kicking them away. She then reached behind her and unclasped the bra to let it fall away. Her nipples were already hard. David knelt down in front of her, put his hands on her hips, and caressed her skin. He planted light kisses on her stomach and licked at her belly button. Then he took her round ass in both of his hands and squeezed.

"God, I missed this body," he said and tugged at her panties to pull them down.

Parker stepped out of the lacy material and automatically spread her legs.

David groaned. "You already know what I want, don't you, baby?"

She moaned in response, obviously anticipating his next move, and he decided not to tease her. He put his face at her pussy, parted the folds with his tongue, and lightly flicked the tiny delicate nub before taking it into his mouth.

* * *

Parker swayed at his first taste, but when his tongue delved deeper, her knees nearly buckled. She braced her hands on his broad shoulders for balance and wound her hips in rhythm to his touch, desperate to get him to taste all of her.

"David," she moaned.

He moaned too but continued his assault on her, licking and sucking as though what she had belonged to him. Combined with the vibrations of his moans, the sounds of his erotic lapping, and the fact that it had just been too damn long, Parker's orgasm came swiftly and with full force. She called out his name, again and again, prolonging the intensity as long as she could, and then finally shuddered and fell against his body.

He didn't allow her to catch her breath for too long, but picked her up, laid her on the bed, spread her legs, and entered her. She watched him as he slid in and out, reacquainting herself with the look on his face as the pressure mounted between them.

"David, please, don't stop!"

She clung to him, her nails digging into his back as he kept his eyes on her. She saw he was close and loved to watch the look that came over him, and it gave her ego a surge to know it was her body that was giving him this pleasure.

"Parker," he said. "Parker!"

Then he closed his eyes and swore to the ceiling. After several moments, the tension left his body, and he looked down at her in a way she couldn't decipher. Was he just as surprised as her that this had happened between them?

Then he lowered himself beside her and pulled her to him to encircle her in his arms, just the way he used to do, and Parker began to breathe easier, relaxing into that safe and secure feeling only he could give her.

CHAPTER SIXTEEN

His vibrating phone is what woke her. After two bouts of sweaty sex, coupled with the adrenaline of last night's events, and the fact that she hadn't received a full night's sleep, Parker was hesitant to open her eyes. But curiosity probed at her. She could feel him leaning toward the nightstand to check the display, and then the bed shifted as he slowly got up. Parker closed her eyes, feigning sleep as he passed by her to enter the adjoining bathroom and soundly shut the door.

Her eyes flew open at the muffled sound of his voice, and she crept out of bed careful not to allow the squeak of the mattress to give her away. She slowly edged to the closed bathroom door and leaned as close as possible. His words were soft, but the one-sided conversation was clear enough.

"I've got Barnes and Somers coming your way. We need to bring her in, David. We're out of time and options."

"I got that," David said, keeping his voice low not to wake Parker.

"We'll keep her in protective custody, but I'll need her to tell us everything she found out from Ian Nelson."

"She's ready to talk. I told her about Nelson. She's upset, but we can use that as motivation to get her to cooperate."

A brief pause, and then his director asked with hesitation, "Were they romantically involved?"

"No," David answered, too quickly. He'd had enough of that topic. If Parker had even the slightest attraction to any other man, he'd spent the better part of the afternoon making her forget it, and he'd enjoyed it very much. The only problem was it made him realize how much he'd missed her.

"Look, I just want to get back to the city, put Gannon away, and end this once and for all."

"All right. Keep her safe until my men get there."

He ended the conversation and powered off his phone. He sat down on the edge of the bathtub and cupped his head in between his hands. He wanted this to be over. He wanted Gannon in a cell, as far away from Parker as possible. He wanted this case closed, so he could go on with his life.

Then what? Would he return to an empty apartment until the next case came along?

He looked to the closed door where, on the other side, his ex-wife lay sleeping. After all this was over, was he willing to let her walk away from him again, or was he making what they shared into something more than just two people in a dangerous situation together?

Sighing heavily under the weight of unresolved emotions, he got up and opened the door slowly. The bed was empty. He looked to his right and saw her standing by the closet, getting dressed. He cleared his throat, wondering how long she'd been awake and if she'd heard any of his conversation.

"Two men from my office will be here to escort us back to San Francisco. We're putting you in protective custody until the trial."

She nodded while pulling her jeans up over her full hips. It made him hard, remembering how he'd gripped them from behind, listening to her moan in pleasure. She fastened her bra, pulled her sweater over her head, and finally faced him. When her eyes connected with his, he knew something had changed.

"Anything else?" she asked.

There was nothing there. No sadness, anger, or joy.

"What's wrong?" he asked.

"Nothing."

"Bullshit. Something happened between the time we fell asleep and now. What—" He stopped himself because, suddenly, he knew what had happened.

She stepped past him to the bedroom door and opened it.

"Parker, I—"

She turned and eyed him, waiting to hear his excuses. But there was nothing left to say. She turned, left the room, and closed the door softly behind her, which was a lot worse than if she'd slammed it.

CHAPTER SEVENTEEN

The rest of the day dragged as the two of them pretended the morning's events never happened. After Parker left him in the bedroom, she went downstairs and pulled out her notes from her interviews with Ian Nelson. She put them on the dining table on top of the surveillance photographs for David to see when he came downstairs.

He must have realized she needed some space from him because he stayed away for nearly a half hour before joining her in the living area. By then, Parker had chosen to relax in front of the TV and check her emotions. If this was all about the job for him, then so be it. It was stupid of her to project this huge fantasy of the two of them getting back together because of a couple of rounds of good sex. They were divorced for a reason. Flipping mindlessly through the channels, Parker tried to remember what that reason was, and if it was even a good enough reason for the two of them not to be together. Growing tired of the shows, she switched off the TV and picked up the newspaper David had bought this morning with breakfast. The front page headline read: *Local Murderer to be Released*. She hadn't been to Gypsy Bay in years and didn't know there was a convicted murderer who lived here.

Parker only got a paragraph into the article before she turned to look over her shoulder and saw David going through the pages of her notes. Putting the paper aside, she stood and walked over to the table, where he read over months of information she and Ian had managed to gather. He glanced up at her for just a moment and then returned to the information. After a while, he shook his head.

"We've had a man in Gannon's organization for nearly two years. He hasn't been able to get even half of what you have here."

She tucked her hands in her back pockets and shrugged. "It wasn't me. Ian gave me everything I needed. I just wrote it down."

He looked up again and must have detected the regret in her tone. "He knew the risks, Parker. He worked for a killer."

She nodded but still couldn't shake the nagging guilt that if Ian had not chosen to seek her out, he might still be alive.

"If it wasn't you, it would have been some other reporter," David said, guessing at her thoughts.

"I suppose so."

It didn't alleviate her guilt or fears, though. Wes Gannon had found out his man turned on him and had him killed, and here she was, awaiting a similar fate. She sat down, braced her elbows on the table, and put her head in her hands.

"What is it?"

She looked up. "I was thinking about those men back at the motel. We were outnumbered, but we got lucky. I'm the only one standing between Gannon and a prison sentence. He's going to send everything he has after me. I probably won't be lucky again."

David closed the file folder and looked straight into her eyes. "Do you think I'd let something happen to you?"

"Not intentionally."

"Not intentionally?"

"I'm scared, okay," she said, her voice rising. "I've done investigative reporting for years, and this is the closest to danger I've been."

His voice went cold. "You should've thought about that."

"Thanks. That helps me a lot."

She stood and marched toward the kitchen and then stopped midway, turned, and glared at him.

"Did it ever occur to you that I took this job because I needed something to fill my time after you walked out?"

"You mean after we lost the baby."

"You said you didn't blame me."

"You think I wanted it to be like this?" he said, now hollering. "You think I want to hide out up here and wait for Gannon or one of his men to make their next move?"

"I compensated you for your time."

"Don't say that."

"Why? It's just sex, and this is just a job for you. That's what you told the director. It's no hardship to spend the weekend with a woman you don't even love as long as you close this case."

That was mean, but she wouldn't take it back. They were both breathing heavily now, exhausted from the yelling and suffocating from despair. David didn't say another word but grabbed his jacket from the armchair and walked out of the house. Parker folded her arms, watching him leave, her pride and ego preventing her from asking him to stay and talk to her. When he slammed the door behind him, she waited a full minute before walking to the front window and sneaking a glance through the curtains. He was inside his car. The dome light was off, but she could still see him through the front windshield. He was sitting in the driver's seat, and his head was down. Parker squinted her eyes as the setting sun turned the day to dusk. Daylight was disappearing, but she saw enough to know he was holding a small piece of paper in his hand. Was that a photograph?

Damn. Why had she let her temper get the best of her like that? Yes, she was scared of what may happen, but not just for herself. Those men knew David had been with her, so he was in as much danger as she was. She wouldn't be able to live with herself if something happened to him because of her desire to pursue a career-making story.

They'd been together for three days now, and the baby had come up twice, while they only circled around the subject when they were married. Maybe if they had just talked about it then instead of burying it, they wouldn't be here now, divorced and screaming at each other. Or maybe they would.

A sound from the kitchen brought Parker out of her daze. She whirled around, but there was nothing there. Maybe it was a raccoon scratching at the back door. She looked back out at David, who was still staring at the picture in his hand. She left the window and headed for the kitchen. She was inches from the doorway of the kitchen when another sound behind her drew her up short. Turning around, her eyes widened, and stark fear raced up her spine at the sight of a large, dangerous-looking man standing in the middle of the living area.

"Who are you?"

He stood there staring at her, one hand resting calmly on the butt of the gun at his waist.

"Get out of here!" Parker backed up slowly and instantly collided into a hard, immovable body. She whipped her head around and then backed away from another man emerging from the kitchen.

For several moments, no one moved or said anything. Parker was in the middle of these two men, looking back and forth between them, waiting for one of them to pounce. They seemed to be waiting for her to do the same.

Closest exit, she thought to herself. The front door. The first big man, who must have climbed in through the upstairs window, was blocking it. The back door through the kitchen was out, too. The stairs. It sounded so cliché, but if she could reach the master bedroom and lock the door, maybe she'd have time to barricade it and get some help. But there could be someone upstairs waiting for her. These men had obviously been clever enough to slip past David, so they no doubt made sure all the exits were blocked. Still, she had to risk it, and not doing anything would surely get her killed.

The man by the kitchen made his first move, diving for her. Parker leaped over the couch out of his way. She grabbed a lamp on the console table and threw it at the window behind the one standing by the front door. That action startled him just seconds enough for Parker to dash by him and run up the stairs. He fired a shot that missed her by inches. Parker screamed but didn't stop running up the stairs, knowing they were right behind her.

CHAPTER EIGHTEEN

David's head snapped up when something crashed against the front window of the house. Fear followed by rage ran through him. Parker was in danger, and he'd left her alone. He reached for the gun at his side and got out of the car, already thinking of a way to get in the house without alerting whoever was inside. But all his plans were halted when he came upon a tall, broad-shouldered figure pointing a gun in his face. David didn't have a chance to blink before the gun fired.

* * *

Heavy booted steps were closing in fast behind her. She had to get to the master bedroom. David had put a spare gun on the nightstand, and she'd have a better chance against two men if she were armed.

She was at the top of the stairs now and turning to race down the hall. In her peripheral vision, she saw one of the men, clothed in black. God, he was so close. What if he shot her in the back? Keep moving! Keep moving! The bedroom door was open, but she didn't think she'd have enough time to get inside and close it behind her. Just as she reached the doorway, he slammed into her from behind, and the two of them fell to the floor. Parker landed on her side, and his heavy weight crushed her shoulder. She cried out from both pain and frustration because the gun was only inches away. She scratched and clawed at him like a wildcat, slapping at his face and hands. He grunted and hollered out when she felt one of her nails dig into his flesh. For that, she was rewarded with a punch to her side. The pain was enough to paralyze her, but she fought through it, kicking at him and doing her best to injure him.

"Bitch," he hollered when she connected with his shin. Parker took great satisfaction in that and then felt something dig into the side of her hip.

His gun. He must have tucked it into his waistband when he ran after her. She raised one forearm to block the heavy blows he tried delivering to her face and used her other hand to reach for his gun. By now they were entangled on the floor, each trying to gain the upper hand, but Parker was no match for his strength, and with the pain racking through her body, she felt herself weakening.

The sound of gunfire outside startled them both. Parker recovered first and used the half second to go for his gun. She gripped the pistol, and he immediately grabbed her wrist and slammed it down hard on the floor over and over until she released it from her grip. She screamed, renewing her efforts to get away from him, but he now had her pinned to the floor. Then more shots came from downstairs.

Oh, God, where was David? Was he hurt? Did they ambush him outside in the car? Parker tried desperately to get away from her attacker, but he used one hand to grasp her neck, holding her immobile and unable to breathe. Then he raised his arm above her with the butt of the gun in his grip, and Parker knew what was coming next.

The blow never came. A single shot fired into the man's forehead, and he seemed to freeze, his eyes wide with surprise, and then glazed over, seeing nothing. Finally, he fell backward with a thud. Parker shimmied her body from underneath his dead weight and was pulled the rest of the way by a pair of strong hands. Tears came to her eyes as she looked up to find David. He gripped her by the forearms and hoisted her up to stand in front of him. Then he pulled her into him for an embrace that felt so good.

"Jesus, I'm so sorry. I shouldn't have left."

"It's okay," she said, muffled against his chest. "I'm fine."

"Did he hurt you?" he asked and allowed her enough breathing room only to get a good look at her.

"Nothing that won't heal."

He looked down at the still body on the carpet and looked ready to put another bullet in him for good measure.

"I heard a gun go off outside," she said, hugging him again fiercely. "I thought they had shot you."

David wrapped his arms tightly around her. "They would have, except the shot you heard was one saving my ass."

Parker pulled back to look at him, a question forming on her lips. It died when she noticed a tall, solidly built man in a uniform striding up behind them.

David turned and nodded at the man. "All clear?"

"My deputies have the one man downstairs in custody." He paused and looked down at the lifeless body. "EMTs are on the way, but I doubt this one will need them."

The man's piercing gaze flashed to Parker. "I'm Sheriff Gray Spencer, ma'am. I'm glad to see you're all right. Agent Holladay nearly got himself killed trying to come rescue you."

Parker realized she was still embracing David, and when

she looked at him, she felt warm inside from the close contact. Still, she slowly released him and shook the sheriff's hand.

"That was you who fired the gun?"

The sheriff nodded.

"I heard the lamp crash against the window," David said. "I was on my way to get you but didn't see one of Gannon's men waiting for me on the other side of the car. The sheriff got him before he got me."

Parker nodded her thanks to Sheriff Spencer and allowed the men to escort her out of the room. Downstairs was a frenzy of sheriff's deputies and the EMTs who had just arrived.

Gray pointed upstairs. "There's a body in the master bedroom." Then he turned back to Parker. "I'd like you to go with the EMTs to the hospital, Ms. Holladay. I know that son of a bitch upstairs had to pull a number on you before we got there. I want to make sure you're okay."

David nodded his agreement, and from the looks on both of their faces, she had no room to argue.

"Just one question," Parker said. "How did you know where to find us? How did you know we were in danger?"

Gray nodded toward David. "His director gave my office a call. He was worried about his men not getting here in time and asked me to come by, introduce myself, and check things out." He paused to take another look around at the activity buzzing around them and shook his head.

"If I'd known it was as serious as all of this, I would have come by sooner. Unfortunately, we've had our own crisis going on here ever since this morning's paper came out."

Parker nodded, remembering the headline. "The local murderer being released next month. I'm sure you've had your hands full with angry and frightened citizens."

Gray's eyes pierced hers, and in them, she saw anger and something else hidden deeper. Something like despair.

A commotion at the front door broke the tension, and the three of them turned to see several men in jackets with DEA stitched on the back crowd into the house. Their escorts back to San Francisco had finally arrived.

CHAPTER NINETEEN

"What the hell is wrong with you?"

Parker's younger sister, Tess, leaned forward in an armchair across the room, glaring at her. It wasn't the first time she'd asked that question.

"I live three miles from that house, and you didn't bother calling me?"

Parker looked away from the TV program she was barely watching and eyed Tess. "The last thing I wanted to do was involve you. You have a four-year-old son. The DEA tells me Gannon's men found us by tracing a call I made to my editor. I would never forgive myself if something happened to you or Justin." She turned and gave her youngest sister, Gretchen, a wink and a smile. "Even you."

Gretchen was sitting in the middle of the living room floor with a giant pizza box in front of her. She returned the smile with an obscene gesture. "I love you more, Parker."

"You still could've called," Tess said. "What if something happened to you?"

"But nothing did happen to me," Parker said, exasperated. "Can't we just focus on that?"

"Thanks to your super cop ex-husband," Gretchen shot back.

The mention of David took Parker back to the events after the catastrophe in Gypsy Bay. She had been taken to the hospital to have her injuries examined, and federal agents and sheriff's deputies were everywhere. But she had been searching for only one man. He came into the hospital exam room after the doctor had given her discharge papers, and she had been relieved to see he hadn't high-tailed it to San Francisco now that she was no longer his problem.

"They're going to take you back to the city and debrief you. They want you in a safe house until Gannon is locked up, given trial, and sentenced. That's not up for debate."

"I wasn't going to argue," she'd said, frowning at his sudden cool and professional tone.

"I made a deal with my director to allow your sisters to stay with you whenever they can. I'm sure you'll want some familiar faces with you."

"Thank you."

He'd gone on to discuss the details of her debriefing, her role in the upcoming trial, and anything else relevant to Gannon's case. However, he tactfully stayed away from any reference to what had transpired between them.

Finally, he'd taken her hand and grasped it. "Thank you, Parker." Then he was gone.

"So, that's it?" Gretchen asked. "He just shook your hand and left?"

Parker shrugged. "What else was he supposed to do?"

Gretchen turned to share a look with Tess before turning back to Parker. "Well, from what you told us about what happened between you two, we figured he'd give you something more than just a handshake."

Parker turned to smile at the two DEA agents playing cards at the dining table and then faced her sisters again. She didn't know how much they'd heard and didn't want anything to get back to David.

"Let's change the subject, please. I'll talk about anything else to get my mind off David, Wes Gannon, and this trial."

They talked well into the night, and by two in the morning, her sisters were asleep in a spare bedroom. Parker had another bedroom all to herself, which she preferred. Growing up, Tess and Gretchen, who were much closer in age, had always shared a room. Being the oldest, Parker had the benefit of her own room, and even though she felt safer with her sisters here, she still welcomed her privacy.

She hadn't been able to sleep and chose to use the quiet time to work on her story. She planned to include all the sordid details of her harrowing experience going up against Gannon's men this weekend. Not only was she reporting this story, but she was also living it, and was going to take full advantage.

She was sitting up in bed, with the pillows propped behind her back, pounding away at the keys on her laptop when she heard muffled voices coming from the living room. She rose from the bed, padded barefoot to the closed door, and put an ear to it. The voices weren't raised, so she opened the door slowly and crept out into the hall. She rounded the corner that led into the living room and stopped when she saw David closing the front door to the agents who'd been watching over her and her sisters. He then turned to face her with his hands deep in the pockets of his jeans. He must have stopped at home to shower and change because his light brown hair was still mussed and damp.

Parker took a step forward. "Gannon?"

"We arrested him about two hours ago."

For the first time in forty-eight hours, she felt like she could take a full breath. "Good. I hope my notes will help."

"That and your testimony."

"Right." Then she frowned. "What did you do with my agents?"

David also took a tentative step forward. "I sent them to get something to eat. I figured they needed a break after watching three women all night. By the way, how are your sisters?"

"Angry with me for not calling them sooner." She paused. "How long will they be gone?"

He stilled at the question, and she took advantage by stepping closer to him, hoping he took the invitation.

"We have one hour," he said, only inches away from her.

"My sisters are asleep."

"Can you be quiet?"

"Yes."

His next move was so fast, she hadn't realized he'd grabbed for her. But before she knew it, he had her turned around and pinned her to him—her back to his front. He was kissing the side of her neck with his hands on her breasts, with his fingers teasing her nipples. Parker grasped the back of his head and tilted her head back, giving him more access. She was so turned on and relieved that he wasn't hurt in the raid to arrest Gannon that she allowed him to touch as much of her as he wanted. She needed to feel his hands all over her, to know he was safe and hers for just a short while. He turned her around and kissed her, moving his hands down to her pajama pants. He yanked them down and cupped her bare ass. He groaned several sexy words into her ear and attacked the buttons of her shirt. He took her breasts in his hands again, and she felt them swell under his touch.

"Don't move," he said, releasing her to pull his shirt over his head and unbutton his jeans.

She didn't have time to fully admire his physique, because he sat on the couch and pulled her to sit astride his lap.

"Ride me, baby," he whispered, grasping her waist.

Parker lowered herself onto him and moved her hips, grinding against his rigid torso.

"David," she said, feeling the pressure building to something wonderful.

"Use me," he said. "I'm all yours." He sucked an erect nipple into his mouth, and the sight of it brought her closer and closer to the edge.

She grabbed the back of his head, urging him to give her more pleasure, while he kept his hands firmly on her waist, guiding her body up and down his shaft.

"Damn," he hissed, increasing their rhythm and building the pressure.

Parker matched his movements, and the two of them reached for release together. When it came, she bit into the pale white flesh of his shoulder to stifle her scream and covered his mouth with her hand. Together, they shared the silent explosion.

* * *

"I owe you an apology. For earlier."

They were lying on the couch, spooned together with a blanket thrown over their naked bodies for warmth. Parker stared straight ahead into the dark screen of the television. She studied their reflections, and it was like looking into a time machine, seeing the way things used to be between them.

"We both said things. You had every right to walk out. You couldn't have known Gannon's men were so close."

"I'm talking about before that. After we… You heard what I said on the phone."

Her shoulders fell and her eyes cast downward. But he must have sensed her immediate withdrawal because he tightened his hold around her waist.

"I don't want you to think this was all a ploy to get you to cooperate with us. Yes, I came to the wedding intending to get you to hand over your notes, but you know I care about you. I was there to make sure nothing happened to you. But everything else…this right here…I wanted you, Parker. It had nothing to do with the job."

She was holding her breath by the time he finished speaking, waiting for him to say what she'd been feeling ever since he'd walked out a year ago. She was still in love with him. But he said nothing else, so she let go the breath filling her lungs.

"Thank you," was all she allowed herself to say.

CHAPTER TWENTY

Three months later…

David stood off to the side of the courthouse steps, away from the cameras and microphones, and watched as a flood of reporters surrounded Parker.

The trial of the U.S. government versus Wesley Gannon had come to an end after fourteen weeks when a grand jury indicted him today on several counts of drug trafficking, murder, and racketeering. With the damning testimony of the DEA's undercover operative and evidence from Parker's notes as well as her own testimony, the verdict had been assured from the beginning. Now, Gannon was facing decades in federal prison, Parker would tell her story, and he would…

David sighed. He would go back to work, secure his promotion, and continue with his life. That's what he'd planned to do since this case began, and he was going to stick to it. Yes, it had been great to get to be near Parker again, even through all the bullshit. It had felt damn good to touch her again.

David straightened as Parker began her brief news

conference. He didn't regret being with her for one second, but it was now over. However, a small voice nagged at him, making him wonder if she felt the same way.

It had rained earlier. Now the sun was beginning to break through the clouds, and a breeze cooled by the rain made its way up the courthouse steps and blew through her hair. Her head was raised high as she gave her statement, looking proud, brave, and to David, she'd never looked more beautiful. Her sisters Tess and Gretchen and her attorney anchored Parker on both sides. David noticed Gretchen not staring into the cameras but looking around for something or someone. Then she saw him and discreetly motioned for him to come stand by them. David shook his head.

The press conference ended, and he watched as Parker was ushered into a waiting car. David stepped forward, trying to see over the crowd surrounding the car. He wanted to make sure she got in and was on her way safely. Just before the door closed, he noticed her looking through the crowd of people, frowning. Then her eyes landed on him. He gave a faint nod, and the door closed before he could see her response. The car drove off, and David cursed himself for not being able to say to her what he wanted.

He loved her and was proud of her.

CHAPTER TWENTY-ONE

Parker read the brass nameplate on the door and smiled.

Deputy Director David Holladay.

She was sitting outside his office, watching as his assistant typed furiously away on the computer. A young man, barely out of college, who Parker learned wanted experience in working in law enforcement without the enforcement part, saying it would help his parents sleep better at night. Parker sympathized in part. She could understand their worry, as she had the same fears when she and David begin dating, but nonetheless, she'd fallen in love with him and married him. She always hated the part of his job where he had to go on drug raids and arrest dangerous criminals and never failed to tell him so.

But three months ago, she'd had a change of heart and had come to respect what he did and the risks he took. No doubt, she wouldn't have survived Gannon's attacks without David being there.

"Parker?"

She'd been staring off into space, so focused on recollections she hadn't heard the door to his office open. Now, he was standing in the doorway dressed in black slacks and a baby blue dress shirt. His badge was clipped to his hip, and she remembered just how fit and strong he was underneath it all.

He gestured toward his office. "Come in."

She rose and nodded her appreciation to his assistant before stepping into his office. It wasn't until then she noticed the look on David's face. Irritation? Anger?

David shut the door behind her and then walked past her, rounding to the back of his desk. "What can I do for you?"

"I came to see how you were. It's been awhile." Almost a month since the trial ended.

He shrugged. "I'm doing fine. Anything else?"

His brusque tone took her aback and had the effect of robbing her of the speech she'd planned. She'd wanted to start this conversation off with small talk, slowly building up to the reasons why they'd had to pretend each other didn't exist, and ultimately the reason she'd broken their unsaid agreement and had come to see him. But his stance, the way he regarded her like a suspect he couldn't wait to arrest, and his dismissive tone all sparked her temper. So this was how it was going to be. Forget the niceties. She wanted to rile him.

"I'm pregnant."

That did it. She watched as the emotionless mask fell away. His eyes slowly widened, his jaw went slack with disbelief, and if it was possible, his skin tone seemed to grow even more pale. He took a step back toward the windows behind his desk. Parker reached into her purse and took out the sonogram photo she'd received from her recent ultrasound and put it on his desk.

"About eight weeks now."

David looked at the picture laid down between them like a gauntlet, and then his eyes flashed on hers, and she knew he was remembering the last time he'd come to see her at the safe house. She thought that first time he came the night Gannon was arrested would be the only time they would see each other. But it turned out he couldn't stay away, and she hadn't wanted him to, no matter how many objections she threw at him.

"We can't keep doing this, David," she said.

He'd wrapped his arms about her waist, fitting himself behind her and nipped at her ear. "Doing what?"

"You know what," she said, feeling the pleasure course down between her legs. "Sneaking around like two teenagers. You could get into trouble. Think about your case."

"I know." He moved down to the crook of her neck. "I tell myself every night I won't come back."

"Why do you?"

He stopped, slowly lifted his head, and turned her around to look at him. "I don't know."

She didn't believe him. He did know; only he didn't want to tell her. Then again, she didn't want to say the words, either. So what did that make her?

He bent his head a little to focus his eyes on hers. "Don't make me leave. I don't want to go back to that empty apartment. Let me stay with you."

When he kissed her again, it was with hesitancy, as though he wasn't sure if she'd welcome it. Parker wrapped her arms around his neck, and the kiss became urgent and desperate. By morning, he was gone, and she didn't see him again until the trial, and even then, it had only been glimpses of him. Apparently, he had meant for that night to be the finale of their adventure together.

David was still silent, eyeing the sonogram as if it were an explosive device.

"I know it's the last thing you need right now," she said. "You just closed a major case, you got a new promotion, and…" She waved a hand to encompass his spacious office. "All of this."

She looked down at her shoes and continued softly. "You're also still mourning Sean."

David reacted like a bullet had struck him. He came from around the desk, his eyes flashing as he advanced on her. "Don't."

Parker didn't back up but stood her ground. "Don't what?"

"Don't say his name."

"Sean," she said. "He was my son, too. He may have been no bigger than the palm of my hand, but he still existed, and I still miss him."

"And this baby is what, your consolation prize?"

"No, you bastard. It's a gift."

Those words seemed to deflate him. The fury had left his eyes, and she was left staring at a man who was hurt and broken.

"I can't go through this again," he said in a near whisper. "I can't feel all of this joy only to have it taken from me. I've gone through it twice already. First with Sean, then with you."

Parker didn't say anything to that. David moved away from her and turned to pick up the picture and stared at it for a long time before looking back at her.

"I left you that morning because, every day, it was getting harder to leave you. We're divorced, Parker, and I knew after the trial we'd go back to our own lives."

"Don't you think this scares me too? I'm the one who pushed myself last time. I'm the one who lost him."

"Stop."

"It's why you left me. You blamed me, so let's not pretend."

"I never blamed you."

"You said—"

"I was being a son of a bitch and fucking selfish. Feeling

sorry for myself. I said it was your fault and then buried myself in work and abandoned you. It was easier than having to accept the fact that I wasn't going to be a father."

"But you are going to be a father."

He moved to one of the chairs in front of his desk and sat down, staring straight ahead.

"That weekend in Phoenix, I felt myself falling for you again. I knew it was happening, but I knew it wasn't good for us."

"So you left?"

"It was for the best."

"And you know what's best for me?"

He came out of the chair. "I know what's best for me, and I can't lose you or our baby again."

It had been the first time since they divorced that he'd spoken his true feelings to her, and it stunned her. It seemed to have stunned him, too, because he simply looked at her. For a long while, they both stared at each other, each weighing what had just been revealed.

A knock sounded at the door, and in the next moment, David's assistant poked his head inside. "Mr. Holladay, I heard shouting—"

"Get out," David commanded, still watching Parker.

The door closed soundly, and David brought his hands to the back of her neck and moved in to kiss her. Parker met him, molding her body against his and wrapping her arms around his neck. They clung to each other, intensifying the kiss, moaning softly as they moved against each other.

Reluctantly, Parker ended the kiss and backed away from him toward the door. "I should let you get back to work."

"Wait," he said, grasping her hand. "I never got a chance to thank you for what you did. The risk you took."

"You thanked me many times."

He shook his head. "It wasn't how I wanted to say it."

She arched a brow. "You're telling me those nights in the safe house with me weren't 'thank yous'?"

"That wasn't thanks. That was I'm horny, and I miss you." He grasped her hand tighter. "Let me take you to dinner."

She thought a moment. "Why don't you pick something up on your way home tonight?"

"Home?"

"Yes. Home. You do remember where our house is, don't you?"

He smiled, and she couldn't help rising up on her heels and meeting his lips again. "Seven-thirty," she said and then turned and headed for the door.

By the time she left the government building and walked out into the afternoon sun, allowing the rays to warm her brown skin. Touching her belly softly, she smiled and said a silent prayer of thanks for their gift. Thinking about David, she said another silent prayer of thanks for second chances.

* * *

Thank you for reading EX FACTOR! If you enjoyed David and Parker's exciting love story, you'll love the next book in the EX FILES series, EXILED.

Gray wants Shannon back in his arms again. But how can he trust her when she confessed to his brother's murder?

ONE-CLICK EXILED NOW >
"Prepare to be wowed."
"This is romantic suspense at its finest."

SIGN UP FOR LISA'S NEWSLETTER:
www.lisaryancampbell.com/newsletter

ABOUT THE AUTHOR

Award-winning Author, Lisa Ryan Campbell began writing as a small child using her mother's pink typewriting paper. Years later, she decided it was important to get a "real job" and attended Arizona State University to major in English with the goal of continuing on for both a Master's and Doctorate degrees in English and teach at the college level.

In 2002, Lisa graduated with a Bachelor's degree in English Literature and an Ancient Egyptian romance novel she wrote in her spare time. She decided then she would not be continuing on to graduate school, but instead joined Romance Writers of America and focused on her true love.

Lisa is an avid traveler and has seen many of the world's treasures in Egypt, Peru, Spain, France, Morocco, England, Mexico and the Caribbean. She spends her time mostly at her home in Colorado writing, reading and watching 1940's noir movies. She also loves to laugh, so you may frequently catch her watching reruns of Archer, Veep and The Office.

Sign up for Lisa's newsletter and find out more about her books at www.Lisaryancampbell.com and connect with her on social media.

9 781958 078020